BIBLIOMANIA

joue, ses inquiétudes, ses angoisses et ses douleurs — il revivait tout en
haletant, étouffé; hors d'haleine — il prenait le livre chéri; il couvrait
ses yeux et le regardait et l'aimait comme un avare son trésor, un
père sa fille, une roi sa couronne —

Cet homme n'avait jamais parlé à personne — il n'était aux bonsjours
et aux bonsoirs — il était distrait et rêveur, sombre et triste — il
n'avait qu'une idée, qu'un amour, qu'une passion : les livres — et
cet amour, cette passion le brûlait intérieurement, usait ses jours, lui
dévorait son existence —

Souvent la nuit, les voisins regardaient à travers les vitres de sa librairie,
une lumière qui vacillait — puis elle s'avançant, s'éloignait, montant,
puis quelquefois elle s'éteignait — alors ils entendaient frapper à leur
porte et c'était Giacomo qui venait rallumer sa bougie qu'une
rafale   avait soufflée.

Ces nuits d'insomnie et brûlantes, il les passait dans ses livres —

Gustave Flaubert

BIBLIOMANIA

A Tale

ILLUSTRATED BY ARTHUR WRAGG

MINIATURE BOOKS

The Rodale Press

ACKNOWLEDGEMENT

The facsimile of the first page of Flaubert's manuscript of *Bibliomanie* which appears on the endpapers is taken from the original in the collection of the late Stefan Zweig, and is reproduced by permission of his heirs.

THIS EDITION PUBLISHED 1954
BY THE RODALE PRESS, 123 NEW BOND STREET, LONDON
AND RODALE BOOKS INC., EMMAUS, PENNSYLVANIA
PRINTED AND BOUND IN ENGLAND
BY MACKAYS OF CHATHAM

FOREWORD

Bibliomanie was written by Gustave Flaubert in November 1836, shortly before his fifteenth birthday. Although he had written a play at the age of ten and was already collecting material for his *Dictionnaire des Idées Reçues** this story was his first published work. It appeared in the edition of 12th February 1837 of *Le Colibri*, a small literary magazine published in Rouen. *Bibliomanie* seems next to have appeared in Flaubert's *Œuvres de jeunesse inédites* which was published as an appendix to his *Œuvres complètes* (Paris, 1910), but it was not until 1926 that the tale was printed on its own, as No. 7 of *Les livrets du bibliophile* (Maestricht, Paris).

There are many legends of the extravagant

* Published in English translation as *A Dictionary of Platitudes,* The Rodale Press, 1954.

lengths to which a book collector will go to get possession of a book which is unique. It is a subject which has always fascinated the French who have usually caste an Englishman or an American as the bibliomaniac, but bibliomania even in these eccentrics was considered to stop well this side of murder. In real life, however, such moderation cannot be relied upon for it was on newspaper reports of the extraordinary case of Don Vincente that the young Flaubert based the plot of his story.

Don Vincente, a Spanish monk, took advantage of the political upheavals of the eighteen-thirties to plunder the libraries of several ancient monasteries including his own monastery of Poplet, near Tarragona. He then disappeared from the view of his clerical superiors to emerge some time later as the proprietor of a bookshop in Barcelona. Don Vincente's consuming passion was to own what he believed to be the only existing copy of the *Furs e ordinacions* printed in 1482 by Lamberto Palmart, the first

6

Spanish printer. On the death of its owner this book was offered at auction and although Don Vincente put up everything he owned he was outbid by Augustino Paxtot, a rival collector. Some nights later Paxtot's house was mysteriously burned down and he died in the flames. Don Vincente's shop was searched and the *Furs e ordinacions* was found there. The bookseller made no attempt to deny his guilt and seemed to be only concerned for the safety of the book. His lawyer was able to establish that another copy of the book existed in Paris and argued from this that it could not be proved that the copy found in Don Vincente's shop was Paxtot's; but he was little aided by his client who moaned loudly 'Alas, alas! My copy is not unique!'

Don Vincente was executed at Barcelona in 1836.

ONCE UPON A TIME THERE LIVED IN A NARROW and sunless street of Barcelona, one of those men with a pale face, dull and sunken eye, one of those satanic and bizarre beings such as Hoffmann dug up in his dreams.

He was Giacomo the bookseller.

Though but thirty years of age, he passed already for old and worn out. His figure was tall, but bent like that of an old man. His hair was long, but white. His hands were strong and sinewy, but dried up and covered with wrinkles. His costume was miserable and ragged. He had an awkward and embarrassed air; his face was

9

pale, sad, ugly and even insignificant. People rarely saw him in the streets, except on the days when they sold rare and curious books at auction. Then he was no longer the same indolent and ridiculous man; his eyes were animated, he ran, walked, stamped his feet; he had difficulty in moderating his joy, his uneasiness, his anguish and his grief. He came home panting, gasping, out of breath; he took the cherished book, devoured it with his eyes, and looked at it and loved it as a miser does his treasure, a father his daughter, a king his crown.

This man had never spoken to anyone, unless it were to the bouquinistes and to the second-hand dealers. He was taciturn and a dreamer, sombre and sad. He had but one idea, but one love, but one passion: books. And this love, this passion burned within him, used up his days, devoured his existence.

Often, in the night, the neighbours saw through the windows of the bookshop a light which wavered, then advanced, retreated, mounted, then sometimes went out. Then they heard a knocking at their door and it was Giacomo coming to relight his candle, which a gust of wind had blown out.

These feverish and burning nights he passed among his books. He ran through the store rooms, he ran through the galleries of his library with ecstasy and delight. Then he stopped, his hair in disorder, his eyes fixed and sparkling. His hands, warm and damp, trembled on touching the wood of the shelves.

He took a book, turned over the leaves, felt the paper, examined the gilding, the cover, the letters, the ink, the folds, and the arrangement of drawings for the word *Finis*. Then he changed its place, put it on a higher shelf, and remained for entire hours looking at its title and form.

He went next to the manuscripts, for they were his cherished children. He took one of them, the oldest, the most used, the dirtiest; he looked at its parchment with love and happiness;

11

he smelt its holy and venerable dust; then his nostrils filled with joy and pride, and a smile came upon his lips.

Oh! he was happy, this man, happy in the midst of all that learning of which he scarcely understood the moral import and the literary value. He was happy, seated among all these books, letting his eyes roam over the lettered backs, the worn pages, the yellowed parchment. He loved knowledge as a blind man loves the day. No! it was not learning that he loved; it was its expression. He loved a book because it was a book; he loved its odour, its form, its title. What he loved in a manuscript was its old illegible date, the bizarre and strange Gothic characters, the heavy gilding which loaded its drawings. It was its pages covered with dust, – dust of which he breathed the sweet and tender perfume with delight. It was this pretty word *Finis*, surrounded with two cupids, carried on a ribbon, supporting themselves on a fountain, engraved on a tomb or reposing in a basket of

flowers between the roses, the golden apples and the blue bouquets.

This passion had entirely absorbed him. He scarcely ate, he no longer slept, but he dreamed whole days and nights of his fixed idea: books. He dreamed of all that a royal library should have of the divine, the sublime and the beautiful, and he dreamed of making for himself as big a library as that of the King. How freely he breathed, how proud and strong he felt, when he cast his eye into the immense galleries where the view was lost in books! He raised his head? Books! He lowered it? Books! To the right, to the left, still more books!

In Barcelona he passed for a strange and infernal man, for a savant or a sorcerer.

Yet he scarcely knew how to read.

Nobody dared speak to him, so severe and pale was his face. He had a wicked and treacherous air, and yet he never touched a child to hurt it. It is true that he never gave anything to charity.

He saved all his money, all his goods, all his emotions for books. He had been a monk and for books he had abandoned God. Later he sacrificed for them that which men hold dearest after their God: money. Then he gave to books that which people treasure next to money: his soul.

For some time now his vigils were longer; people saw still later in the night his lamp which burned on his books, meaning that he had a new treasure, a manuscript.

One morning, there came into his shop a young student of Salamanca. He seemed to be rich, for two footmen held his mule at Giacomo's door. He had a toque of red velvet, and rings shone on his fingers.

He did not have, however, that air of sufficiency and of nullity usual with people who have bedecked valets, fine clothes and an empty head. No, this man was a savant, but a rich savant. That is to say a man who, at Paris, writes on a mahogany desk, has books gilded on the edges, embroidered slippers, a dressing-gown, Chinese curiosities, a gilt clock, a cat that sleeps on a rug, and two or three women who make him read his verses, his prose and his tales, who say to him: 'You have ability,' – and who find him only a fop.

The manners of this gentleman were polished. On entering, he saluted the bookseller, made a profound bow, and said to him in an affable tone:

'Do you not have here some manuscripts?'

The bookseller became embarrassed and replied stammering:

'Why, sir, who told you that?'

'Nobody, but I imagine it.'

And he put down on the desk of the bookseller a purse full of gold, which he made resound, smiling as does everyone who touches gold of which he is the owner.

'Sir,' replied Giacomo, 'it is true that I have some, but I do not sell them. I keep them.'

'And why? What do you do with them?'

"Why, my lord?' – and he became red with anger – 'You ask what I do with them? Oh, no, you do not know what a manuscript is!'

'Pardon, Master Giacomo, I am posted on it and to give you the proof of it I will tell you that you have here the *Chronicle of Turkey*!'

'I? Oh, they have deceived you, my lord!'

'No, Giacomo,' replied the gentleman. 'Re-assure yourself, I do not at all want to rob you, but to buy it from you.'

'Never!'

'Oh, you will sell it to me,' replied the scholar, 'for you have it here. It was sold at Ricciami's the day of his death.'

'Well, then, yes, sir, I have it. It is my trea-sure: it is my life. Oh! you will not snatch it from me! Listen! I am going to confide a secret in you: Baptisto, you know Baptisto, the book-seller, my rival and my enemy, who lives in the Palace Square? Well, then, he does not have it, not he, but I do have it!'

'At how much do you value it?'

Giacomo stopped a long time and replied with a proud air:

'Two hundred pistoles, my lord.'

He looked at the young man with a triumphant air, as if he were saying to him: 'You are going to leave; it's too high, and yet I will not give it for less.'

He was mistaken, for the other man, showing his purse, said:

'There are three hundred.'

Giacomo turned pale, and almost fainted.

'Three hundred pistoles?' he repeated. 'But I am a fool, my lord, I will not sell it for four hundred.'

The student began to laugh, fumbling in his pocket, from which he drew out two other purses.

'Well, then, Giacomo, here are five hundred. Oh, no, you do not want to sell it, Giacomo, but I will have it. I will have it to-day, this instant. I need it. If I had to sell this ring given with a kiss, if I had to sell my sword studded with diamonds, my houses and my palaces, if I had to sell my soul, I must have this book. Yes, I must have it at all costs, at any price. In a week I am defending a thesis at Salamanca. I need this book to become a doctor. I must be a doctor to be an archbishop. I need the purple gown before I can have the tiara on my forehead.'

Giacomo approached him with admiration and respect as the only man whom he had understood.

'Listen, Giacomo,' interrupted the nobleman. 'I am going to tell you a secret which is going to make your fortune and your happiness. There is a man here who lives at the Arabs' Gate. He has a book: it is the *Mystery of Saint Michael.*'

'The *Mystery of Saint Michael*?' said Giacomo, raising a cry of joy. 'Oh, thanks! You have saved my life!'

'Quick! Give me the *Chronicle of Turkey.*'

Giacomo ran to a shelf. There he suddenly

stopped, – turned pale, – and said with an astonished air:

'But, my lord, I do not have it.'

'Oh, Giacomo, that is a very clumsy trick, and your looks belie your words.'

'Oh, my lord, I swear to you, I do not have it.'

'Why, you are an old fool, Giacomo. Look, here are six hundred pistoles.'

Giacomo took the manuscript and gave it to the young man.

'Take care of it,' said he, when the other man went off laughing and said to his valets as he mounted his mule:

'You know that your master is a fool, but he has just deceived an imbecile. The idiot of a churlish monk!' he repeated laughing. 'He believes that I am going to be Pope!'

And the poor Giacomo remained sad and disconsolate, leaning his burning forehead on the window panes of his shop, weeping with rage and regarding with bitterness and grief his manuscript, the object of his care and of his affection, which the gross footmen of the nobleman were carrying away.

'Oh, accursed man of hell! accursed, a hundred times accursed are you who have robbed me of all that I love on earth! Oh, I cannot live now! I know that he has deceived me, the infamous one, he has deceived me! If this be so, I shall avenge myself. Let us go quickly to the Arabs' Gate. If this man were to ask me a sum larger than I have, what to do then? Oh, it is enough to kill one!'

He took the money which the student had left on the desk and went out running.

While he was going through the streets he saw nothing of all that surrounded him. Everything passed before him like a nightmare, of which he did not understand the enigma. He heard neither the feet of the passers-by nor the noise of the wheels on the paving. He did not think, he did not dream, he did not see anything but books. He was thinking of the *Mystery of*

Saint Michael. He fashioned it to himself, in his imagination, large and thin, with parchment ornamented with gold letters. He tried to guess the number of pages which it must contain. His heart beat with violence like that of a man who awaits his death sentence.

At last he arrived. The student had not deceived him. On an old Persian carpet, full of holes, were laid out on the ground some ten books. Giacomo, without speaking to the man who, stretched out like his books, was sleeping at one side and snoring in the sun, fell on his knees and began to cast an uneasy and anxious eye over the backs of the books. Then he arose, pale and crestfallen, and wakened the bouquiniste with a shout and asked him:

'Ah, friend, you do not have here the *Mystery of Saint Michael*?'

'What?' said the merchant opening his eyes, 'you do not mean to speak about a book which I have? Look around for yourself!'

'The imbecile!' said Giacomo, kicking him

with his foot. 'Have you others than these?'

'Yes, let's see, here they are.'

And he showed him a little packet of pamphlets tied with cords. Giacomo broke the cords, and read the titles of them in a second.

'Hell,' said he, 'it is not that. Have you not sold it perhaps? Oh, if you have got it, give it, give it! One hundred pistoles, two hundred, all that you wish!'

The bouquiniste looked at him astonished:

'Oh! perhaps you mean to speak of a little book which I gave yesterday for eight maravedis to the curé of the Cathedral of Oviedo?'

'Do you remember the title of this book?'

'No.'

'Was it not the *Mystery of Saint Michael*?'

'Yes, that's it.'

Giacomo turned away a few steps and fell in the dust like a man worn out by an apparition which possesses him.

When he came to himself, it was evening and the sun which reddened the horizon was in its decline. He raised himself and went home sick and despairing.

A week later, Giacomo had not forgotten the sad disappointment and his wound was still throbbing and bleeding. He had not slept at all for three nights, for this day there was to be sold the first book which had been printed in Spain, a copy unique in the kingdom. It was a long time that he had wanted to have it. So he was happy the day that they told him that the owner was now dead.

But an uneasiness seized his spirit. Baptisto could buy it, Baptisto who for some time had taken from him, not the customers, – that concerned him very little, – but all that which appeared rare and old, – Baptisto whose fame he hated with the hatred of an artist. This man became burdensome to him, it was always he who took away the manuscripts. At public sales he bid and he obtained. Oh! how many times the poor monk, in his dreams of ambition and of pride, how many times he saw come toward him Baptisto's long hand which passed across the crowd as on the days of a sale, come to rob him of a treasure of which he had dreamed so long, which he had coveted with so much love and egotism! How many times also had he been tempted to end with a crime that which neither money nor patience had been able to accomplish. But he drove back this idea in his heart, tried to divert his thoughts from the hatred which he bore to this man and went to sleep on his books.

Early in the morning he was in front of the house in which the sale was to take place. He was there before the auctioneer, before the public and before the sun.

As soon as the doors opened he precipitated himself in the stairway, went into the room and asked for this book. They showed it to him. That was already a happiness.

Oh! never had he seen anything so beautiful or that pleased him more! It was a Latin Bible, with Greek commentaries. He looked at it and

admired it more than all the others. He clasped it between his fingers, smiling bitterly, like a man who is starving in sight of gold.

Never, moreover, had he desired anything so much. Oh! how he coveted it then, even at the price of all that which he had, his books, his manuscripts, his six hundred pistoles, at the price of his blood. Oh! how he would have liked to have this book! To sell all, all to have this book, to have only it, but to have it for himself, to be able to show to all Spain, with a smile of insult and pity for the King, for the princes, for the savants, for Baptisto, and say: 'Mine, this book is mine!' and to hold it in his two hands all his life, to fondle it as he touches it, to take in all its fragrance as he smells it!

At last the hour arrived. Baptisto was in the centre, with serene face, calm and peaceful air. They came to the book. Giacomo offered at first twenty pistoles. Baptisto kept quiet and did not look at the Bible. Already the monk

advanced his hand to seize this book, which
had cost him no little trouble and anguish,
when Baptisto started to say:

'Forty!'

Giacomo saw with horror that his antagonist
got excited in proportion as the price mounted
higher.

'Fifty!' he cried with all his strength.

'Sixty!' replied Baptisto.

'One hundred!'

'Four hundred!'

'Five hundred!' added the monk regretfully.

And while he stamped his feet with im-
patience and anger, Baptisto affected an ironical
and wicked calmness. Already the sharp and
cracked voice of the usher had repeated three
times: 'Five hundred.' Already Giacomo was
consumed with happiness. A sigh which
escaped from the lips of a man came near caus-
ing him to faint, for the bookseller of the Palace
Square, pressing forward in the crowd, said:

'Six hundred!' The voice of the usher

repeated four times: 'Six hundred' – and no other voice replied to him. Only there was seen at one end of the table, a man with pale forehead, with trembling hands, a man who laughed bitterly with that laugh of the damned in Dante. He lowered his head, thrust his hand in his chest and when he withdrew it, it was warm and moist, for he had flesh and blood at the end of his finger nails.

They passed the book from hand to hand, so as to bring it within reach of Baptisto. The book passed before Giacomo. He smelled its fragrance; he saw it pass an instant before his eyes, then stop before a man who took it laughing. Then the monk lowered his head to hide his face, for he was weeping. On returning by the streets, his walk was slow and painful. His face was strange and stupid, his figure grotesque and ridiculous. He had the air of an intoxicated man, for he staggered. His eyes were half closed; he had red and burning eyelids. The perspiration ran down his forehead and he stammered between his teeth, like a man who has drunk too much and who has partaken too freely at a banquet. His thought was no longer under control; it wavered like his body, without having either end or intention; it was unsettled, irresolute, heavy and bizarre. His head weighed like lead, his forehead burned like a brazier.

Yes, he was drunk with that which he had felt, he was fatigued with his days and he was surfeited with existence. That day – it was a Sunday – the people promenaded in the streets, talking and singing. The poor monk listened to their chatting and their songs. He gathered in the road some scraps of phrases, some words, some cries, but it seemed to him that it was always the same sound, the same voice. It was a vague, confused hubbub, a music bizarre and noisy, which buzzed in his head and which crushed him.

'Say,' said one man to his neighbour, 'have you heard tell of the story of that poor curé of

Oviedo who was found strangled in his bed?'

Here, there was a group of women who took the evening air on their doorsteps. Here is what Giacomo heard in passing before them:

'Say then, Martha, do you know that there was at Salamanca, a rich young man, Don Bernardo, – you know, the one who, when he came here a few days ago, had a fine black mule, so pretty and so well equipped, and who made it paw the paving stones? Well, then, the poor young man, they told me at church this morning, that he was dead!'

'Dead?' said a young girl.

'Yes, little one,' replied the woman. 'He is dead, here, at the Hotel de Saint-Pierre. First he felt bad in his head; then he had a fever, and at the end of four days they buried him.'

Giacomo heard still other things. All these souvenirs made him tremble, and a ferocious smile came to play around his mouth.

The monk went home, worn out and sick. He stretched out on the bench of his desk and slept.

His chest was oppressed; a raucous and hollow sound came from his throat. He awoke with fever. A horrible nightmare had exhausted his strength.

It was then night and it had just struck eleven at the neighbouring church. Giacomo heard cries of 'Fire! Fire!' He opened his windows, went into the street and actually saw flames which shot up above the roofs. He went back and was going to take up his lamp to go into his shop when he heard before his windows men running past and saying: 'It is in the Palace Square. The fire is at Baptisto's!'

The monk gave a start; a loud peal of laughter rose from the depths of his heart, and he proceeded with the crowd towards the bookseller's house. The house was on fire; the flames rose up, high and terrible, and driven by the winds, they darted towards the fine blue sky of Spain which looked down on agitated and tumultuous Barcelona like a veil covering up tears. They saw a man half naked; he was

E

desperate; he was tearing his hair; he rolled on the ground, blaspheming God and raising cries of rage and despair. It was Baptisto.

The monk contemplated his despair and his cries with calmness and happiness, with that wild laughter of the child laughing at the tortures of the butterfly whose wings he has plucked.

They saw in an upper story flames which were burning some bundles of paper. Giacomo took a ladder, leaned it against the blackened and tottering wall. The ladder trembled under his steps. He mounted on a run, and arrived at that window. Curses! It was nothing but some old books from the bookshop, without value or merit. What to do? He had entered; it was necessary either to advance in the midst of this inflamed atmosphere or to descend again by the ladder of which the wood was beginning to get hot. No! He advanced.

He crossed several rooms; the floor trembled under his steps; the doors fell when he approached them; the beams hung down over his

E*

head; he ran into the midst of the fire, panting and furious.

He needed that book! He must have it or death!

He did not know where to direct his course, but he ran.

At last he arrived before a partition, which was intact. He broke it with a kick and saw an obscure and narrow apartment. He groped, he felt some books under his fingers. He touched one of them, took it and carried it away out of this room. It was it! it, the *Mystery of Saint Michael*! He retraced his steps, like a man lost and in delirium. He leaped over the holes; he flew into the flame, but he did not find again the ladder which he had placed against the wall. He came to a window and descended outside, clinging with hands and knees to the rough surfaces. His clothing began to get on fire and when he arrived in the street he rolled himself in the gutter to put out the flames which were burning him.

SOME MONTHS PASSED AND ONE NO LONGER
heard talk about the bookseller Giacomo,
except as one of those singular and strange men
at whom the crowd laughs in the streets because it does not at all understand their pas-
sions and their manias.

Spain was occupied with more grave and
more serious interests. An evil genius seemed
to be hanging over it. Each day, new murders
and new crimes, and all seemed to come from
an invisible and hidden hand. It was a dagger
suspended over every roof and over every
family. There were people who disappeared

37

suddenly without any trace of blood spilled from their wound. A man started out on a journey; he never came back. They did not know to what to attribute this horrible scourge, for it is necessary to attribute misfortune to some one who is a stranger, but happiness to oneself. In fact there are days so ill-omened in life, epochs so baneful to men, that not knowing whom to crush with his maledictions one cries out to heaven. It is during these unfortunate epochs for the people that one believes in fatality.

A quick and industrious police had tried, it is true, to discover the author of all these crimes. The hired spy had slipped into all the houses, had listened to all the words, heard all the cries, seen all the looks, – and had learned nothing. The Prosecutor had opened all the letters, broken all the seals, searched in all the corners, and had found nothing.

One morning, however, Barcelona had left off its robe of mourning to crowd into the

Courts of Justice where they were going to condemn to death the man whom they supposed to be the author of all these horrible murders. The people hid their tears under a convulsive laugh, for when one suffers and when one weeps, it is a consolation, self-centred it is true, to see the sufferings and tears of others.

Poor Giacomo, so calm and so peaceful, was accused of having burned the house of Baptisto, of having stolen his Bible. He was charged also with a thousand other accusations. He was there, seated on the bench for murderers and brigands. He, the honest bibliophile, the poor Giacomo, who thought only of his books, was now compromised in the mysteries of murder and the scaffold.

The room was glutted with people. At last the Prosecutor raised himself and read his report. He was long and diffuse; it was with difficulty that one could distinguish the principal action from parentheses and reflections.

39

The Prosecutor said that he had found in the house of Giacomo the Bible which belonged to Baptisto, since this Bible was the only one of its kind in Spain; now it was probable that it was Giacomo who had set fire to the house of Baptisto to possess himself of this rare and precious book. He stopped and seated himself, out of breath.

As to the monk, he was calm and undisturbed and did not reply even by a look to the multitude which was insulting him.

His advocate rose, spoke long and well. Then, when he believed he had shaken his audience, he raised his robe and drew out from it a book. He opened it and showed it to the public. It was another copy of this same Bible.

Giacomo raised a cry and fell back on his bench, tearing his hair. The moment was critical. A word from the accused was awaited, but no sound came from his mouth. At last he seated himself, looked at his judges and at his attorney like a man who is just wakening.

They asked him if he were guilty of having set fire to the house of Baptisto.

'No, alas!' he replied.

'No?'

'But are you going to condemn me? Oh! condemn me, I beg of you! Life is a burden to me. My attorney has lied to you. Do not believe him. Oh, condemn me! I have killed Don Bernardo, I have killed the curé, I have stolen the book, the unique book, for there are not two of them in Spain! My lords, kill me! I am a miserable wretch!'

His attorney came towards him and, showing him this Bible, said:

'I can save you, look!'

Giacomo took the book, and looked at it.

'Oh, I who believed that it was the only one in Spain! Oh, tell me, tell me that you have deceived me! May misfortune attend you!'

And he fell in a faint.

The judges returned and pronounced the sentence of death upon him.

Giacomo heard it without a shudder and he seemed calmer and more tranquil.

They gave him hope that by asking pardon from the Pope he would perhaps obtain it. He did not wish it at all, and asked only that his library be given to the man who had the most books in Spain.

Then, when the people had dispersed, he asked his attorney to have the goodness to loan him this book. The man gave it to him. Giacomo took it lovingly, dropped some tears on the leaves, then tore it with anger, and threw its fragments at the person of his defender, saying to him:

'You have lied about it, mister attorney! I told you truly that it was the only copy in Spain!'

Bibliomanie

Bibliomanie

—————

Dans une rue étroite et sans soleil de Barcelone vivait il y a
peu de temps un de ces hommes au front pâle, à l'œil terne, creux,
un de ces êtres sataniques et bizarres tels que Hoffmann en déterrait
dans ses rêves.

C'était Giacomo, le libraire. — Il avait trente ans et il passait
déjà pour vieux et usé. — Sa taille était haute mais courbée comme
celle d'un vieillard. — Ses cheveux étaient longs mais blancs. — Ses
mains étaient fortes et nerveuses, mais desséchées et couvertes de
rides. — Son costume était misérable et déguenillé. — Il avait l'air
gauche et embarrassé. — Sa physionomie était pâle, triste, laide
et même insignifiante. —

Ne le voyait rarement dans les rues, si ce n'est le jour où l'on
vendrait à l'enchère des livres rares et curieux — alors ce n'était plus